A Gift For:

From:

Copyright © 2018 Hallmark Licensing, LLC

Published by Hallmark Gift Books,
a division of Hallmark Cards, Inc.,
Kansas City, MO 64141
Visit us on the Web at Hallmark.com.

All rights reserved. No part of this publication may be reproduced, transmitted, or stored in any form or by any means without the prior written permission of the publisher.

Art Director: Chris Opheim
Designer: Ren-Whei Harn
Production Designer: Dan Horton

ISBN: 978-1-63059-683-5
1BOK1345

Made in China
1118

What Does a Big Brother Do?

By Delia Berrigan
Illustrated by Lizzie Walkley

A new baby is coming!

Have you heard the news?

You're going to be a Big Brother!

But wait.

What exactly does a Big Brother do?

He is the new baby's very first friend.

They will get to learn, grow, and play together.

They'll read stories and play pretend!

They'll get to go on all kinds of adventures.

You know, a Big Brother used to be a baby, too.

So he knows just what a baby needs.

His parents will need his help!
Babies can't do a lot for themselves,
so parents are very busy.

Big Brothers can help feed the baby. Big Brothers can show the baby how he feeds himself!

He can help change and bathe the baby, too!

Big Brothers can show babies how to take a nap.

What else does a Big Brother do?

Most of all, a Big Brother is loved—

so very, very loved.

You are loved by all those around you

and especially by the new baby!

If you enjoyed this book
or it has touched your life in some way,
we'd love to hear from you.

Please write a review at Hallmark.com,
e-mail us at booknotes@hallmark.com,
or send your comments to:

Hallmark Book Feedback
P.O. Box 419034
Mail Drop 100
Kansas City, MO 64141